For my wife, Teri, who keeps me a kid at heart

Rosie & Rex: A Nose for Fun

For information address HarperCollins Children's Books, a division of HarperCollins Publishers,
10 East 53rd Street, New York, NY 10022.
www.harpercollinschildrens.com

Library of Congress Cataloging-in-Publication Data is available.
ISBN 978-0-06-221131-6

The artist used his imagination, four years of art school, and Photoshop
to create the digital illustrations for this book.
Typography by Rachel Zegar
13 14 15 16 17   SCP   10 9 8 7 6 5 4 3 2 1
❖
First Edition

ROSIE & REX
A Nose for Fun!

Hi, Rosie!

Written and illustrated by Bob Boyle

HARPER
An Imprint of HarperCollinsPublishers

Let's play princess ballerina tea party!

Maybe it's a vase for
pretty-pretty flowers!

Maybe it's a super special sippy cup.

Maybe it's a bird feeder!

Birds are fun,
but . . .

I'VE BEEN LOOKING FOR MY NOSE ALL DAY!

DO YOU WANT TO DO SOMETHING FUN? HOW ABOUT A . . .

Robots ARE fun!

I think it's a
fancy new dress!

Or a supersonic
downhill slider!

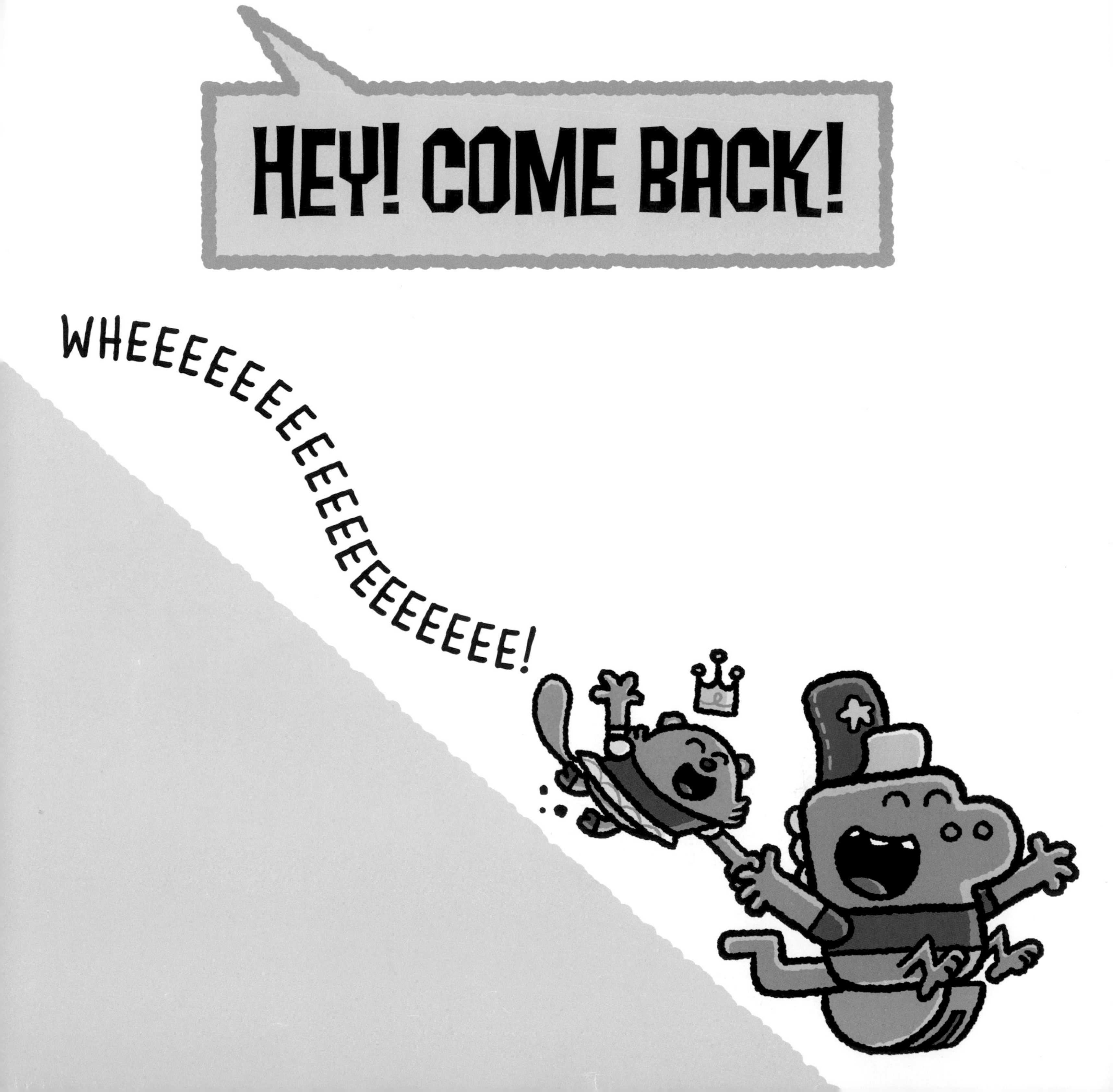
HEY! COME BACK!
WHEEEEEEEEEEEEEEEEEEE!

THAT'S MY EAR!